SMILE for the Camera!

Dear Reader

When we use a camera to capture special moments, we can thank many clever inventors from the past – many of whom are featured on pages 6–9. And if you enjoy using your digital camera, read about its inventor on pages 10–11.

UNDERWATER CAMERAS HELP SWIMMERS TO ANALYSE AND IMPROVE THEIR SWIMMING FOR COMPETITIONS.

When writing this book, I also had the pleasure of meeting a young photographer, Belinda Janke, who prefers to use film cameras when taking photographs. Her photographs were so unique and eye-catching I just had to include her work in this book. View Belinda's photography on pages 22–31.

I hope you enjoy tracing the development of camera technology and seeing how that technology has been adapted for a range of uses today.

Sharon Parsons

My sincere thanks to the following people for their time, information, images and enthusiasm for this book:

Belinda Janke, Toowoomba, Australia

Andy Cross, Toowoomba, Australia

Ryan Bennett, Swimpro Cameras, Melbourne, Australia

Andy Cross, Brisbane, Australia

NELSON
CENGAGE Learning™
For learning solutions, visit **cengage.com.au**

Contents

SMILE for the Camera!

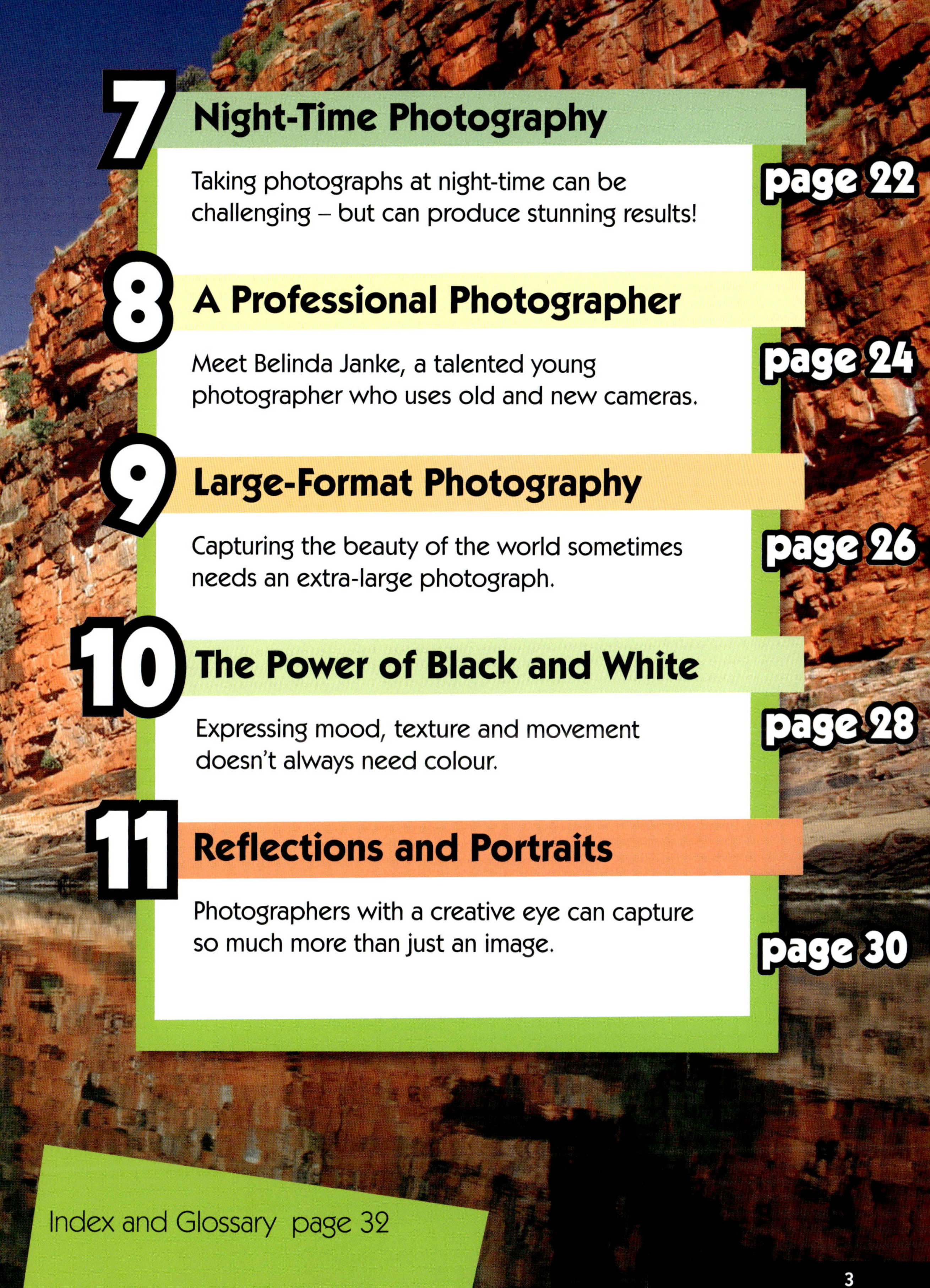

1 Capturing Images in the Past

Before cameras were invented, people had to have their pictures painted by artists who were called "miniature portrait painters", or "miniaturists". This time-consuming process was expensive, so only wealthy people and members of royal families could afford miniature portraits.

Miniature portraits were especially popular between the 1500s and the 1700s. The miniaturists were in demand and during that time thousands of portraits were painted.

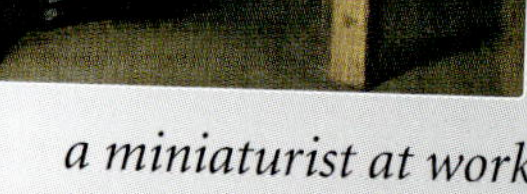

a miniaturist at work

George Engleheart

a typical miniature portrait

Arts

A Famous Miniature Portrait Painter

George Engleheart (1750–1829) was one of the England's most famous miniaturists. During his 39-year-career, George painted 4 853 portraits of important people of the time, some many times. For example, he painted King George III 25 times!

Cumbersome Cameras

For many years, scientists and inventors discovered all kinds of information to help them build photographic devices. But most inventions for early cameras were complex and impractical for everyday use. By the 1800s, however, the French had invented important technology that enabled other inventors to create more useful and easy-to-use cameras.

Try fitting this into your pocket!

This camera unfolded from its own wooden suitcase.

2 The History of Cameras

Below is a timeline featuring some of the scientists and inventors who made significant contributions to the invention of cameras throughout history.

1827: Frenchman Joseph Niepce (1765–1833) created the first photographic images, which were called sun prints. But the images took eight hours of exposure and they faded after some time.

Joseph Niepce

1837: Frenchman Louis-Jacques-Mandé Daguerre (1787–1851), who had briefly worked with Niepce, invented the first photographic process, called the "daguerreotype". Each image only took half an hour of exposure to develop.

Louis-Jacques-Mandé Daguerre

Turning Point

The French government bought the rights to the daguerreotype process from Daguerre and announced that the technology was free for anyone to use!

1841: Englishman William Talbot (1800–1877) invented the positive/negative process used in photographic development, called the "calotype" (or "talbotype") process.

daguerreotype

an image produced using the calotype process

Turning Point

Talbot licensed his new process to a portrait miniaturist painter. Soon miniaturists were not as popular as in previous years.

1861: Scottish scientist and mathematician James Maxwell (1831–1879) created the first true colour photograph.

1885: American George Eastman (1854–1932) created photographic film to help process photographs more quickly.

Turning Point

In 1888, Eastman's Kodak Company released the first box camera for everyone to use. He called it a Kodak – a camera brand still available today.

James Maxwell

George Eastman taking a photograph with a Kodak box camera

a Kodak box camera

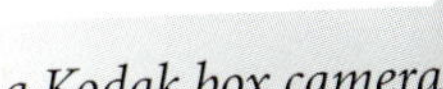

> YOU PRESS THE BUTTON, WE DO THE REST.
>
> GEORGE EASTMAN

Old cameras were large and cumbersome.

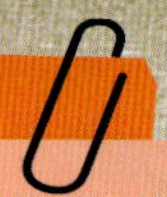

1900: George Eastman also invented the first snapshot-type camera called the Brownie. It was very successful up until the 1960s.

1948: American Edwin Land (1909–1991) invented the first Polaroid camera. People were amazed that a photograph could be instantly produced.

History

Kindness at Kodak

When George Eastman became very wealthy from sales of cameras and film, he gave a gift of extra money to each employee in 1899. Then he set up a "Wage Dividend" so that each employee got more than their wages; they also received a share of the company's profits every year.

Edwin Land

an early polaroid camera

1975: American Steven Sasson, who was working for Kodak, invented the first digital camera. He also took the first digital image.

1991: Kodak mass-produced the first digital camera.

2001: Kodak released a more affordable digital camera for everyone. From that time, digital cameras became very popular and were readily available from many different companies.

Steven Sasson

an early digital camera

3 The First Digital Camera Design

Steven Sasson was working for Kodak as an electrical engineer when he invented the first digital camera. In 1974, Steven's manager asked him to try and build a camera using a new electronic sensor called a charge-coupled device (CCD). The CCD captured light and optical information.

Steven was very excited about this great opportunity to invent a filmless camera.

"Wouldn't it be amazing to build an electronic camera with no moving parts?" he thought to himself.

Steven Sasson began the process by sketching a camera design on a white sheet of paper.

Then he asked his lab technicians to help him build the toaster-sized camera with circuit boards, a steel frame, a box and a lens. After one year, Steven tested it and took the first digital image. The image showed Steven that he had to make some final adjustments, which he did, and soon after, the image was perfect. By 1976, the first digital camera, with a playback device and TV screen, was ready to be presented to Steven's manager and the team at Kodak. Several years later, a new digital camera was made for people to buy.

US President Barack Obama makes a presentation to Steven Sasson for his contribution to camera technology.

CAMERA LENS PROFESSIONAL

Camera and Cassette

The prototype of the digital camera stored binary digital data like a computer does.

It took 23 seconds to store the image data, as the camera was only 0.01 megapixels.

CAMERA LENS PROFESSIONAL

Playback Device

The digital camera had a cassette reader to play the cassette. It took 23 seconds to load the image data to make the images ready to be seen on a TV screen.

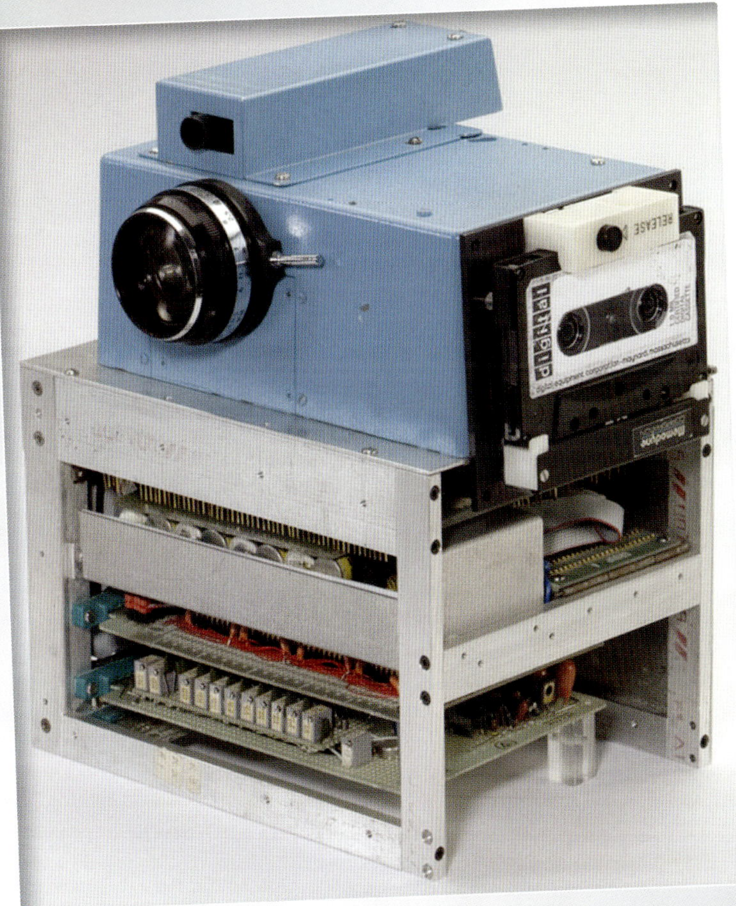

Steven Sasson's first digital camera

CAMERA LENS PROFESSIONAL

TV Screen

The data was transferred from the playback device to the TV set via a video signal.

4 Digital and Film Camera Technology

To understand how a digital camera works, let's compare it to a film camera. The main difference is that digital cameras use a tiny in-built computer and the images are stored electronically on a memory card. Film cameras use film to "store" the images, and you cannot see the image until you receive the photographs as prints after they have been developed. In the days when only film cameras were available, seeing the developed photos was either a surprise or a shock!

a digital camera

a high-quality film camera, called a Wisner technical camera

Technology

Film Cameras

To see the photos from film cameras, people take rolls of film (inside a light-proof container) to a film processer, who develops the images and prints them onto special paper in a darkroom environment. This process was initially completed by hand, but film-developing machines now make the processing of camera film much quicker.

Differences Between Digital and Film Cameras

Compare the differences between a digital camera and film camera below. The only similarity between the two camera types is that they both need light to enter the camera lens.

Digital Camera	Film Camera
Light enters the camera lens and strikes electronic sensors behind the lens.	Light enters the camera lens and strikes a film covered in chemicals behind the lens.
The sensors convert the electronic signals into a digital image made up of pixels. A computer chip arranges the pixels so you can see the image on the view screen.	A chemical reaction between the light and the chemicals creates a negative "copy" of the image on the film's surface.
Images are stored on a memory card. Later, they can be downloaded onto a computer to be edited or printed on a home printer or at a digital printing store.	Negative film is taken to a film-processing store to be developed. Copies of the negatives are turned into photographs. Negatives must be used for every copy.
Images can be viewed digitally on the camera before they are downloaded, or on a computer, digital photo frame or on television after they have been downloaded.	Photographs are placed into book-format photo albums or in frames. Negatives must also be stored safely if more copies are required later.

A **Digital** Camera's Flash

In a digital camera, a built-in electronic flash provides a light source when there is not enough light. The camera's flash sensors make some adjustments so the image will be clear.

Technology

Get Rid of Red-Eye

Sometimes people look like they have red eyes in a photograph. This occurs when light from a camera's flash reflects off tissue at the back of the eye. You can edit the red-eye out on your computer, or avoid it by fitting a larger flash to the camera.

Using a **Film** Camera

Andy Cross is a photographer who prefers to use a high-quality technical camera, called a Wisner, because he believes it can produce a sharper image than a digital camera.

Andy has set up the camera for the shot.

Andy checks the scene carefully before taking the photograph.

The image can only be viewed upside down.

the developed photograph

Read more about film cameras in Chapter 8.

5 A Review of Kids' Digital Cameras

It's one month before my birthday and my grandparents want to buy me a new digital camera. When they were my age, they used an ancient camera called a Brownie. That was many years ago, before digital cameras. They have a digital camera now but they don't know much about the best cameras for kids, so they have asked me to do some research on the Internet before we go shopping. My budget is $100. I found a website that has reviews about lots of different cameras written by kids and camera experts. It has a colourful chart with information that compares each camera. The chart helped me to quickly work out my top three cameras. They look really cool, too – that helps!

After I read everything on the website, I was able to choose my top three cameras – the Kiddz 3-D Zoom, Apps-Zoom and the All Star 3-D.

We spent ages at the camera store, but it was worth it to find exactly the right camera for me. I worked out that although I really like the 3-D cameras, I don't need one just yet. Instead, for my requirements, the Apps-Zoom is the best because it looks cool and has loads of modes and apps. What's the best feature? It's waterproof, so that when I go surfing I can take some shots. My grandparents looked happy as they paid for my birthday present. I'm a lucky kid! I can't wait to take lots of photos.

Kids' Digital Cameras (8–12 years old)

Rating Key
4 Stars = Best
3 Stars = Good
2 Stars = Average
1 Star = Below Average

	Kiddz 3-D Zoom	Kiddz Tuff	Apps-Zoom	Gee-Zoom	Gee-Apps-Galore	All Star 3-D
Price	$59.95	$36.50	$73.95	$44.50	$24.95	$39.95
Overall rating	★★★★	★★★½	★★★½	★★★½	★★★	★★★
Ratings						
Design features	★★★★	★★★½	★★★½	★★★	★★★½	★★★
Specifications	★★★★	★★★★	★★★½	★★★½	★★½	★★★
Usability	★★★★	★★★★	★★★½	★★★½	★★★	★★★
Customer service	★★★★	★★★½	★★★½	★★★½	★★★	★★★
Design Features						
Resolution (megapixels)	2	1.3	1.3	1.3	1.3	0.3
Optical zoom					✓	
Flash	✓	✓	✓	✓		✓
Playback mode	✓	✓	✓	✓		✓
Camcorder mode	✓				✓	
Photo editing	✓	✓	✓	✓		✓
Specifications						
Built-in memory capacity	256MB	128MB	32MB	64MB	2MB	8MB
Battery type	AA	AAA	AA	AAA	AAA	AAA
Display screen (inches)	1.8	1.44	1.5	1.5	1	1.5
Usability						
Warranty	1 year	1 year	1 year	1 year	1 year	1 year
Customer Service						
Help available	✓	✓	✓	✓	✓	✓

6 High-Speed Cameras

PROFESSIONAL CAMERA LENS

85mm 1:1.4D

On the Roads

Many companies around the world manufacture speed cameras and other traffic enforcement technology, such as red-light cameras. Speed-camera technology helps police to identify drivers who speed beyond the legal limit. As a deterrent, people who speed are fined, and it is hoped that they will not speed any more. This technology is designed to help keep people safe from speeding and dangerous drivers.

Speed cameras monitor and capture drivers who exceed the speed limit.

a border speed sign in Germany

Road Speed Limits

Speed limits are imposed in most places to maintain safety on different road surfaces and environments.

In 1861, the first speed limit was introduced in the United Kingdom – 16 km per hour.

In Germany, an advisory speed (130 km per hour) is suggested for travel on the autobahns. The autobahn is one of the longest motorway systems in the world.

Speed cameras can take photographs of the driver and the car's number plate, too.

Cameras Test Turbulence

New aircraft designs are tested in wind tunnels to check how the air flows around each part of the aircraft at high speeds. Researchers use film cameras, high-speed cameras and strobe lights to help capture the effects of turbulence on parts of the aircraft. If the aircraft suffers from too much turbulence, the design can be adapted to minimise the effects of this powerful force. High-speed cameras in the wind tunnels also capture stop-motion images of fast-moving parts, such as aircraft propellers, to check if they are functioning correctly and safely.

a photograph taken to test the effects of turbulence on an aircraft prototype

Physical Science

What Causes Turbulence?

Turbulence is air movement that can occur in certain weather conditions, such as jet streams, thunderstorms and atmospheric pressures. When aircraft fly into turbulent weather, pilots always caution passengers to sit down and fasten seatbelts because turbulence is the leading cause of in-flight injuries.

Cameras in Sport

High-speed camera technology is used at the Olympic Games and other sporting championships to accurately record finishing times.

Swimming Pool Cameras

Special underwater camera systems are often used by swimmers and their coaches at sports institutes.

Each camera system has a telescopic camera that is attached to a swimming pool wall or floor by a bracket system. The camera can be remote-controlled to swivel, and it can be adjusted to shoot footage of the swimmer at any angle.

Swimmers and sports institutes also use the camera system as a training tool because it provides instant feedback on style and technique.

The footage is transmitted to a hard drive on a laptop computer and can be shown on a very large television screen for instant review.

an underwater camera is used at a swimming rac

images from the camera appear on a television screen

the underwater camera in the pool

That's a close finish!

Capturing Close Finishes

The finish-line cameras are so sophisticated that they can shoot thousands of frames per second. Their accuracy can provide finish-time results to the nearest one-hundred-thousandth of a second!

Glory at the 2000 Olympic Games for Steven Redgrave!

Setting Rowing Records

At the elite level of international rowing competitions, rowers must race for a distance of 2000 metres. Rowing times are mostly affected by weather conditions.

Biography Snapshot

British rower Steven Redgrave (1962–) is one the greatest rowers of all time. He began rowing when he was 17 years old and has won many championships.

Steven has participated in five Olympic Games (1984, 1988, 1992, 1996, 2000) and won gold medals at every event. He is the only rower to have won gold medals at five consecutive Olympic Games events. He retired in the year 2000.

7 Night-Time Photography

PROFESSIONAL CAMERA LENS

Belinda Janke is a talented young photographer who lives in Toowoomba, Queensland. She will travel almost anywhere to capture amazing images and that is exactly what she did one night.

Deep in the Springbrook rainforest on the Gold Coast, Queensland, Belinda lugged her camera and tripod over rocks and logs to photograph glowing mushrooms.

85mm 1:1.4D

Belinda Janke used a digital camera to photograph the glowing mushrooms.

SPRINGBROOK RESEARCH CENTRE

The Springbrook Research Centre is based in a rainforest on the Gold Coast in Queensland. Among other things, the staff educate visitors about living things that glow.

In wet, tropical areas, some fungus species glow in the dark. This is due to a chemical process that occurs within the fungus called "bioluminescence", where energy is given off in the form of light.

Glowing Periods at Springbrook

	Jan.	Feb.	Mar.	Apr.	May	Jun.	Jul.	Aug.	Sep.	Oct.	Nov.	Dec.
Fireflies											●	●
Luminous Mushrooms	●	●	●								●	●
Glow-worms (← Breeding Period →)	●	●	●	●	●	●	●	●	●	●	●	●

MUSHROOMS, THE SIZE OF DINNER PLATES!

BELINDA JANKE, PHOTOGRAPHER

Most mushrooms grow to about five centimetres in diameter.

a glowing mushroom

Long Exposure

To capture images of these amazing glowing mushrooms at night-time, long exposure is the ideal camera technique. It requires the photographer to keep the camera shutter open for longer – about 10 to 30 seconds. A longer exposure produces a brighter image.

Long exposure is the camera technique that captured the mushrooms' bright-green colour.

Luminous Mushroom Propagation

Springbrook Research Centre has a successful luminous mushroom propagation program in their Luminous Garden. Fascinated visitors can see more luminance in one area than they would see in the natural environment.

8 A Professional Photographer

CAMERA LENS PROFESSIONAL

From Jillaroo to Photographer

Photographer Belinda Janke used to work as a jillaroo in the Northern Territory, Australia. Her work involved mustering cattle on ranches, and it was this experience in the outback that inspired her to explore photography. Today, Belinda works as a professional photographer and a graphic designer.

Belinda mustering cattle in the Northern Territory, Australia

Belinda taking a photograph using a film camera

Belinda relaxing after a hard day mustering cattle

jillaroo: A young woman who works on a sheep or cattle station

mustering: The act of gathering together animals on farms for things like shearing or moving to another location

Belinda Prefers Film Photography

Belinda Janke uses digital cameras for some photography work, but she prefers to use a film camera, such as a Wisner technical camera. Look at Belinda's images below to compare the same scene photographed in colour and in black and white.

Belinda likes using Andy's Wisner camera

Belinda's Photography Lesson

Belinda gets help from her photography teacher and mentor, Andy Cross.

Black and White or Colour?

Belinda prefers this black and white photograph (taken with the Wisner) because it produced a sharper image.

Belinda took this colour image with a digital camera.

9 Large-Format Photography

Belinda's Photographs

"Large-format photography" is a type of photography sometimes used when taking photos of landscapes and images that will be enlarged and need to show a high level of detail.

A large-format camera is used, usually with a 4 x 5 inch (about 10 x 12 centimetres) sized film. Digital cameras can also be used for large-format photography.

Belinda enjoys using the Wisner camera to capture wide-format landscape images.

A DARKROOM

A darkroom is a pitch-black room used by photographers to develop photographic film. Developing photos in a darkroom gives the photographer greater control over how photographs will look.

Belinda's large-format photograph of a long camel train

Long Jetty, a town in NSW, at sunset

a photographer working in a darkroom

Large-format photography produces crisp colours in the outback.

Galvin Gorge, the Kimberleys, in Western Australia

Large-format photography produces incredibly clear and detailed images of landscapes.

10 The Power of Black and White

Black and **White** Effects

Taking photographs in black and white produces images with a variety of tones and contrasts that sometimes are not possible to see in colour photographs. View some of Belinda's amazing black and white photographs, taken with her film camera, on these two pages.

Cropped Shots of Fast Flowing Water

This photo shows the contrasts of black and white tones of rocks and fast-flowing water.

A strong, clean, precise shot is a photographer's ideal outcome for a black and white image.

Sharp contrasts between the movement of the waterfall and the bold rocks are visible in this shot.

Texture and Movement of the Subject

Many different textures can be seen in this photograph, as well as the movement of the water.

11 Reflections and Portraits

An Eye For **Reflections**

Photographers must have a good eye for creativity to capture memorable images. Using reflections in photography is one technique to produce an eye-catching image. Belinda focusses on a water reflection to create a unique work of art.

Belinda has photographed the reflection of the trees onto water to create this stunning image.

Portraits with Smiles

Belinda enjoys taking portrait images of babies and young children in both black and white and in colour. As well as photographing their facial expression, Belinda tries to capture her subject's personality as well.

a portrait taken with the right amount of light and at the right angle

Candid portraits involve good timing.

focus on personality for maximum effect

Index

Glossary

bioluminescence The production of light by a living organism, where energy is released by a chemical reaction in the organism's body

darkroom A room that can be made completely dark to allow the processing of light-sensitive materials, like photographic film

exposure The total amount of light allowed to fall on the camera film or sensor while taking a photograph

jillaroo A young woman who works on a sheep or cattle station

mustering The act of gathering together animals on farms for things like shearing or moving to another location

photographic studio A place where a photographer takes, develops or prints photographs. It may include a darkroom.

pixel A very small element of colour, that when put together, makes a graphic image. The more pixels there are in an image, the greater its resolution.

portraiture The art of taking a photographic portrait of a person, to capture their face and facial expressions

prototype An original form of something that is tested so that the design can be changed before the product is manufactured and sold

reflection When light is bent or thrown back from a surface. In photography, using reflections from water, windows or mirrors can produce beautiful, artistic images.